Jonatha
Ghost

Jonathan struggled to make sense of it all.

'So what you're telling me is, you were killed by a bomb in the war. World War Two?'

'That's right. Rotten luck really, it was just near the end.'

'Then what are you doing here?'

'I'm a ghost aren't I?' said the boy reasonably. 'I mean it stands to reason.'

Reasonable was just what it wasn't, thought Jonathan. 'But ... well, what's it like? Being dead?'

'Dead boring.'

Jonathan's Ghost

by

Terrance Dicks

Illustrated by
Adriano Gon

RED FOX

A Red Fox Book
Published by Random Century Children's Books
20 Vauxhall Bridge Road, London SW1V 2SA
A division of the Random Century Group

London Melbourne Sydney Auckland
Johannesburg and agencies throughout
the world

First published by Piccadilly Press 1988

Red Fox edition 1990
Reprinted 1990 and 1991·

Text © Terrance Dicks 1988

Printed and bound in Great Britain by
The Guernsey Press Co Ltd
Guernsey, C.I.

ISBN 0 09 968730 5

CHAPTER ONE

Noises in the Night

Suddenly Jonathan woke up.

Somewhere in the distance a clock began chiming the hours. Instinctively, Jonathan counted the strokes. One . . . two . . . three . . . four . . . five . . . six . . . seven . . . eight . . . nine . . . ten . . . eleven . . . twelve!

As the sound of the last stroke faded away, there was a sort of scuffling sound from the darkest corner of the big room.

Jonathan sat up in bed, eyes wide, hair standing on end.

It was midnight.

He was in a haunted house.

And there was someone in his room.

1

Someone or something . . .

Jonathan stared hard into the dark corner, trying to convince himself he was imagining things, that he'd imagined the noises that had woken him up.

But he hadn't.

There was another, louder this time.

And there in the darkness a shape was beginning to form. A very surprising one.

Jonathan had been expecting the usual hooded, sheeted form, or maybe someone in old-fashioned clothes with his head tucked underneath his arm.

But this apparition was surprising because it was so ordinary.

It was in the shape of a boy – a boy of very much Jonathan's own age. And yet – there was something very odd about this boy. His clothes for instance.

He was wearing short trousers for a start. Grey flannel shorts, baggy ones, held up by a striped cricket belt with an S-shaped snake clasp.

As well as the shorts he wore a sleeveless V-necked pullover, a grey shirt with a stringy-looking striped tie, and a school blazer. A school cap was stuck on the back of his head.

The other odd thing about the boy was that you could see right through him. At least, you

could and you couldn't . . . He seemed to be getting more and more solid every minute.

He came out of the shadows and stood at the end of Jonathan's bed, grinning cheekily at him. "Wanna play?"

Jonathan stared at him, too astonished to speak.

"How about a game of hide and seek?" said the strange boy.

He turned and ran towards the bedroom wall.

He ran straight through it and disappeared.

Jonathan did what any normal red-blooded boy would do in the circumstances.

He sat bolt upright in bed and roared, "Mum! Dad! I've just seen a ghost!"

There were footsteps in the corridor and his parents dashed in, both fully dressed, both tired and dusty. They'd moved into their new house that very day, and they were still wrestling with the unpacking.

"What's the matter?" said his dad crossly.

More sympathetically, his mother said, "What's up? Are you all right?"

Suddenly Jonathan found he didn't want to go into details. They probably wouldn't believe him anyway.

"Sorry," he said sheepishly. "I must have been having some sort of nightmare. I thought I saw something."

His father turned on the light and looked round the room. "Well, there's no-one here now, is there?"

"I expect you're just over-tired," said his

mother. "No wonder after the day we've had. Do you want me to stay with you for a bit?"

"No, that's all right." Already Jonathan felt a bit ashamed about having made such a fuss. Perhaps he really had had a nightmare and imagined everything. "You'd better get to bed yourself, you look worn out."

Jonathan's dad, who was really very kind beneath the grumpiness, patted him on the shoulder. "Don't worry, son, anyone can have a bad dream. See you tomorrow. Want me to leave the light on?"

"No, that's okay."

Jonathan's parents said their goodnights and went off, turning the light out and closing the door behind them.

Jonathan lay there in the darkness, wide awake and thinking . . .

It was bad enough having to move, without being haunted as well.

Jonathan's father worked for a firm of sweet manufacturers, and he'd worked his way up to being manager of their factory in Norwich.

Then, suddenly, he'd been promoted to Head Office.

It meant more money and a bigger company car. That was the good news.

The bad news was that Head Office was in London and the whole family would have to move.

Jonathan's mother would have to change her job – she was a part-time accountant and book-keeper – and they'd have to find a new house, though the company would help with that.

For Jonathan it meant leaving his school and all his friends. To make matters worse, he'd not long changed from junior to senior school anyway and was just getting settled.

Now he had to do it all over again.

Jonathan was an only child and a bit of a loner anyway. He found the idea of a new house and a new school all at once pretty daunting.

The house was a big old-fashioned one in a pleasant London suburb, a nice area with shops and a school and an underground station all nearby.

The house was the only one in the street standing empty, and the estate agent said they were lucky to get it. "If it wasn't for this

silly rumour about it being haunted it would have been snapped up long ago."

Pressed for details he'd admitted that the previous occupants had been bothered with noises in the night, mysteriously broken cups and plates and things like that. Jonathan's mother had been a bit worried, but Jonathan's dad wasn't superstitious in the least. He didn't believe in ghosts and the house was much the best one that they'd been offered. So they took it.

Jonathan's father had laughed when he first heard the story about the house being haunted.

Jonathan had laughed too at the time.

But that was in a nice well-lit room with other people around. Now, in a darkened room at midnight it didn't seem so funny.

Still, it had been a tiring day, and Jonathan felt himself getting sleepy.

Perhaps it had all been a nightmare after all.

Jonathan felt himself starting to drift into sleep.

Then a voice said, "Sorry about all that fuss!"

Suddenly wide awake, Jonathan sat up.

The strange boy was sitting on the end of the bed.

He looked quite real and solid this time, just an ordinary scruffy-looking boy.

Funnily enough, Jonathan didn't feel particularly scared.

More indignant, really. "Look, what are you doing in my room?"

"My room as well, innit? At least, half of it is, the other half copped it when I did."

"What do you mean?"

The boy pointed to the big, square window. "All that lot's new. This used to be an attic

8

with just a tiny window. My bed was just there. One night a doodlebug scored a direct hit on the house next door – and knocked the top off our house as well."

"Doodlebug?"

"Yeah, you know, a buzz-bomb. Sort of a robot bomb with wings, no pilot. Jerry sent them over."

"Jerry?"

"Germans. Nasties. Old Hitler's mob. Don't you know anything?"

Jonathan struggled to make sense of it all. "So what you're telling me is, you were killed by a bomb in the war. World War Two?"

"That's right. Rotten luck, really, it was just near the end."

"Then what are you doing here?"

"I'm a ghost, aren't I?" said the boy reasonably. "I mean, it stands to reason."

Reasonable was just what it wasn't, thought Jonathan. "But . . . well, what's it like? Being dead?"

"Dead boring."

"What about . . . well, Heaven and all that?"

"Well, would you fancy it? Everything all

spick and span, angels, choir practice . . .
That's why some of us – pop back, see what's
going on. You miss it, being alive."

"Don't they mind?"

"Well, they're not mad about it. But they
turn a blind eye. Glad to be rid of us, I reckon.
What's your name?"

"Jonathan. Jonathan Dent."

The boy put out a grimy hand. "Dave
Morris. Shake."

Jonathan put his hand out. Solemnly they
shook hands.

Dave's hand felt strong and sinewy, and
utterly real.

Suddenly the light went on and Jonathan's mother's voice said, "What on earth are you doing?"

She was standing in the doorway in her dressing-gown. "I just looked in to see if you were all right . . ."

Well she'll have to believe me now, thought Jonathan, now that she's seen for herself.

But there was nothing to see.

Nobody was sitting on the end of the bed and Jonathan was shaking hands with empty air.

"Are you all right?" asked his mother anxiously. "Why are you sitting up?"

Jonathan felt a real twit. "I'm fine, I must have been sleep-sitting!"

His mother came and tucked him in. "Well, stop all this nonsense and go to sleep. You've got your new school in the morning."

She turned the light out and went off.

Jonathan snuggled down under the covers. Soon, despite himself, he felt himself dozing off.

Just before he dropped off he thought he heard a voice say, "Goodnight, mate."

"'Night," murmured Jonathan sleepily.

At least he'd made one new friend, he thought as he drifted off. Even if that friend was a ghost . . .

CHAPTER TWO
The Haunted Classroom

Everyone overslept the next morning, the day started in a mad rush, and Jonathan just didn't have time to think over what had happened.

After a hasty wash, dress and breakfast, his mother drove him to his new school, and Jonathan found himself facing his new headmaster.

To his astonishment the Head was a still-youngish man in a rumpled, tweed sports jacket. He wore big horn-rimmed glasses and had wildly untidy hair.

"I know how you feel," he said briskly, "I'm a new boy here myself. You know it's only a couple of days till the end of term? Don't suppose you'll learn much before then, we're starting to wind down already, what with the School Match, concerts, exhibitions, that sort of thing. Still, at least you'll meet your new class, find your feet a bit, start afresh next term."

He handed Jonathan over to a tall prefect who took him off to meet his new form master and his new form.

His new form master was called Mr Fox and he was red-haired and rather foxy-looking himself. "Sit at the back, there, trail round with the others, we'll get you sorted out over the next few days."

He consulted a timetable. "Right, maths first, with me – mental arithmetic test to get the old brains buzzing."

Everyone groaned. Jonathan learned later that these impromptu tests were a great favourite with Mr Fox, who was a firm believer in the old-fashioned times-table methods. Everyone in the class hated them and demanded to know why they couldn't use calculators like everyone else.

Mr Fox passed round scrap paper and

pencils and started yelling out questions. "Seven times eight?"

A voice in Jonathan's ear whispered, "Fifty-six," and instinctively he wrote it down.

"Nine sevens?"

"Sixty-three," said the voice, and again Jonathan wrote it straight down.

He looked up and saw Dave sitting on his desk.

Immediately last night's events came flooding back. "Here, what are you – "

"No talking during the test," yelled Mr Fox. "Sixty-eight divided by seventeen?"

Dave winked and said, "Easy. Four!"

Jonathan shrugged and put the answer down.

After the test – there were twenty questions in all – Mr Fox called out the answer and you had to swap papers with your neighbour for marking.

A beefy, tough-looking boy was sitting nearest to Jonathan. He snatched Jonathan's paper away and dumped his own scrawled one in front of him.

To Jonathan's astonishment he took absolutely no notice of David, who was still perched on the desk.

When the marking was over you had to swap papers back and call out your own score.

The majority of people got scores of around the ten out of twenty level, only one or two getting as many as fifteen or sixteen. The beefy-looking boy was last but one to call out his score – he only got three out of twenty. "See me after school, Briggs," said Mr Fox. "A little extra practice for you." He turned to Jonathan. "Now, what about you, Dent?"

Jonathan looked down at his paper and blinked.

"Never mind if it's lowish," said Mr Fox

kindly. "These little tests of mine take some getting used to. What did you get – how many answers right?"

"Er – all of them, sir."

"What?" Mr Fox whizzed down the aisle. "Let me see that paper!"

He snatched it from Jonathan's desk and scanned it rapidly. "Good grief! We appear to have an Einstein in our midst! Arithmetic your best subject, Dent?"

"Not really, sir," said Jonathan truthfully. He crossed his fingers under his desk. "The maths teacher at my last school used to give tests like that too, so I just got used to them."

After all, he thought, he could hardly tell the truth . . .

As Mr Fox turned away, Jonathan looked up at David and hissed, "What do you think you're up to?"

"Just trying to help, mate," said David. "We had those tests all the time, I just thought I'd give you a hand. Want to make a good impression, don't we?"

"Not by cheating, we don't. You'll just get me in trouble!"

"Sorry!" David gave him an offended look

18

and vanished.

To Jonathan's relief there was no sign of him during the rest of the lesson, nor during the next one, which was history. (Perhaps it wasn't one of his good subjects, thought Jonathan.)

After that it was break time.

As he followed the others out of the classroom, Jonathan noticed that the beefy boy, Briggs was glaring at him.

As Briggs disappeared through the door a small bespectacled boy with big ears sidled up to Jonathan. "I wouldn't go out there if I were you!"

"Why not?"

"Well, you gave Briggsy a low mark, didn't you? Three out of twenty."

"That's all he got right."

"You just don't understand our local customs. If you're marking Basher Briggsy's papers, you give him a decent mark – whatever he gets! It's not healthy if you don't. He'll be waiting for you now."

"Let him," said Jonathan, with more courage than he felt. He didn't want any trouble, but he wasn't going to skulk indoors

on his first day.

"Best of luck," said the bespectacled little boy. "My name's Timothy, by the way. Tiny Tim, or Lugs, for obvious reasons. Take your pick."

"How about if I just call you Timothy?"

Timothy showed him the way to the noisy, crowded playground, and sure enough, Basher Briggs, surrounded by a few cronies, loomed up straight away. "Here! I want a word with you!"

Jonathan thought it best to say nothing.

Briggs towered over him, breathing heavily. "I ought to pulverise you," he announced. "But I'm giving you a chance 'cos you're new, see, just this once. Next time you mark one of my papers you give me a decent mark – not *too* high, but not too low either. Or else!" He flourished a big fist under Jonathan's nose.

Still Jonathan didn't say anything. With a final glare, Briggs turned away.

Jonathan heaved a sigh of relief. Maybe he hadn't been very heroic, but he hadn't got flattened either.

Then to his horror a now-familiar voice said, "We're not standing for that, are we?"

David was standing beside him. Cupping his hands around his mouth he yelled after the retreating Briggs. "Go and take a running jump, fatty!" Then he vanished.

Briggs whirled round. "*What* did you say?"

"Nothing," said Jonathan hurriedly. "Not a word."

Briggs gave him a suspicious look, then

21

turned away again.

Immediately, David reappeared. Dashing up to the retreating Briggs, he delivered the most tremendous kick to the backside – and then vanished again.

So when Briggs swung round with a roar of rage, there was only Jonathan to be seen.

"Right!" snarled Briggs. "You're dead!" Raising his fists, he dashed at Jonathan like an express train.

A yell of "Fight! Fight! Fight!" went up and a crowd surrounded them.

Jonathan gulped and put up his fists, thinking he might as well die fighting.

Then, just as Briggs reached him, something very odd happened.

Briggs went, "Oof!" and staggered back, clutching his tummy.

He attacked again, fists whirling.

Then he yelled, "Ouch!" and clutched at his eye. And "Argh!" and grabbed at his nose which suddenly started bleeding.

Dazed with pain and rage he flung a wild punch which brushed the end of Jonathan's nose.

Jonathan swung a couple of even wilder

punches which missed Briggs by inches.

The effect was amazing!

Briggs staggered back under a whirlwind of invisible blows, then crashed to the ground.

Instinctively, Jonathan went to help him.

To his astonishment, Briggs cowered away. "All right, all right, I've had enough!"

He lay there snivelling, trying to wipe the tears from his eye and the blood from his nose at the same time, and only succeeding in smearing a mixture of both over his face till he looked like something from a horror movie.

The circle of boys looked at Jonathan with awed respect. "Look at the mess he made of old Briggsy," whispered one of them. "And not a mark on him – he's not even breathing hard."

"That's right," agreed his equally astonished friend. "Some of those punches were so fast I didn't even see his fist move!"

Suddenly, the crowd started to melt away, and Jonathan turned and saw Mr Fox, who happened to be on playground duty.

He looked at the prostrate Briggs and then

at Jonathan.

"Well, Dent, you haven't lost much time in making your mark – especially on poor old Briggs here." He heaved Briggs to his feet. "Go to the toilets and clean yourself up, Briggs – and in future be more careful who you pick on!" As Briggs hurried away, Mr Fox turned back to Jonathan, who was adopting his usual tactic of keeping quiet.

"You don't have to say anything, boy, I'm well aware of Briggs's little ways." He looked thoughtfully at Jonathan. "You could be quite an asset to this class. I must say, I'm all agog to see what you'll get up to next!"

"So am I, sir," said Jonathan without thinking.

Mr Fox gave him a thoughtful look and turned away.

David suddenly appeared, gave Jonathan a thumbs-up sign and disappeared.

Jonathan sighed.

Something told him there was a lot more trouble in store. And he was right!

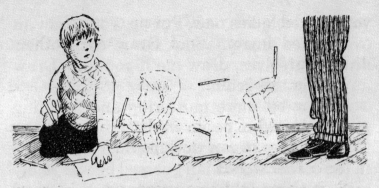

CHAPTER THREE

The Invisible Artist

There was a double art period after break, which meant that Jonathan got a chance to tuck himself away in a quiet corner and do some sketching. At least, that was the idea . . .

The art master, a fiery Welshman called Huw Hughes, issued big pads and lots of pencils, and said art couldn't be taught anyway so they'd just have to get on with it. "Draw me a portrait!"

"Who are we to draw, sir?" asked someone.

"Anyone you like, boy . . . "

Someone in the front row started sketching furiously and Huw Hughes boomed, "None of your naked ladies now, Purvis. You've got an overheated imagination. Draw each other, draw yourselves, draw me if you like. Draw anyone in this room!"

After a bit more muttering and fidgeting people started to get to work.

Mr Hughes began working on a big canvas in the corner. Jonathan guessed he was really more of an artist than an art teacher, and had probably only taken the job to earn eating money till he became world famous.

Jonathan stared at the blank sheet of paper, trying to think what to draw. He was still too stirred up by the events of the morning to concentrate.

Suddenly Dave appeared beside him. "Do one of that potty teacher then," he suggested helpfully. "Sort of a cartoon. I was good at cartoons when I was at school."

"Sssh, he'll hear you," whispered Jonathan.

"Oh no he won't," said Dave confidently.

He went up to Mr Hughes, stepped in front of him, put his thumb to his nose and wiggled his fingers furiously and yelled, "Yah, boo, sucks, potty old pencil-pusher!"

Mr Hughes took no notice, and neither did anyone else. "See?" said Dave triumphantly, and came back to Jonathan.

"I don't get it." said Jonathan. "Sometimes you're invisible, right? But sometimes I can see and hear you – but nobody else seems to."

"You can only see me when I materialise," explained David. "It's hard work, materialising, takes it right out of you. Can't keep it up all that long either."

"But why is it that when you materialise, nobody seems to see or hear you but me?"

"Listen mate, we ghosts don't appear to just anybody, you know. You have to be *sensitive*. Either that, or there has to be some kind of special link."

"You mean like people seeing the ghosts of their grannies, that sort of thing?"

"That's it."

"So what's the link between us then? I mean, I don't think I'm sensitive, you're the first ghost I've ever seen, and I don't think we're related or anything."

Dave looked hurt. "You're my best mate, aren't you?"

"Am I?"

"Course you are. We're like them two geezers in the Bible, David and Jonathan. I knew we'd be pals as soon as I heard your name." He looked anxiously at Jonathan. "We are mates, aren't we?"

Suddenly Jonathan realised that the ghost must be very lonely. 'Yes, of course we're mates," said Jonathan. "Best mates."

They shook hands and there was a little silence.

"Listen," said Jonathan. "When you're invisible, right? You can still sort of affect people?"

"I affected that fat bully who tried to bash you, didn't I?"

Jonathan was trying to get some idea of his new friend's powers – he thought it might be safe if he knew exactly what Dave could and couldn't do. "What about things . . . objects. Can you move them as well?"

"Watch," said Dave and disappeared again.

Suddenly one of the pencils on David's table rose up in the air, floating in space before him.

"Oy!" said Jonathan, and grabbed it back.

Another pencil rose in the air, hovering over the pad.

"All right, all right, give it back," said Jonathan.

Suddenly a long bony hand clamped down on his shoulder. "And just what do you think you're up to, boyo? Juggling with our pencils are we – and babbling away to ourselves . . . I know all artists are mad, but don't overdo it!"

Suddenly, Jonathan realised that although nobody could see Dave, everybody could see *him.* See him talking to himself, or surrounded by floating objects. If he wasn't careful, Dave was going to land him in a lot of trouble.

Desperately Jonathan tried to think of something more believable than the truth. "I often talk to myself when I'm working sir, don't you? And fiddling with things helps me to concentrate on my work."

Even as he said it, it sounded pretty feeble, and Mr Hughes thought so as well.

"Work?" he yelled. "What work? I've had my eye on you for quite a while, boy, and you haven't drawn so much as a line."

He snatched Jonathan's pad and turned it round – and gasped.

Jonathan gasped too, though his gasp was one of pure horror.

On the pad was a sort of cartoon portrait in thick black pencil. Mr Hughes was tall and thin and beaky nosed and the cartoon showed him as an ostrich – an ostrich that was somehow unmistakably Huw Hughes.

Mr Hughes studied the drawing. "Said you could do a portrait of me, didn't I?"

"You didn't say what kind of portrait," said

Jonathan hopefully.

"No, I didn't insist on it being flattering, did I?" He aimed a mock cuff at David's head. "This is pretty good, actually. Though what beats me is how you did it so quick . . ."

"Just a knack," said Jonathan modestly.

Huw Hughes looked thoughtfully at him. Jonathan realised that lots of people were looking at him that way this morning.

Mr Hughes said, "You're the new kid, aren't you? Mr Fox was talking about you in the staff-room just after break, sounds to me like you're a bit of a wizard. You want to watch your step, boyo, or I might just have you exorcised!"

To Jonathan's relief, he turned and went back to his painting.

By lunchtime, Jonathan was turning into the school celebrity. Everyone in the class had crowded round for a look at the cartoon of Huw Hughes as an ostrich, and this, together with his defeat of Briggs and the hundred per cent score in the test made people think he must be some kind of prodigy.

All through lunch, Jonathan could feel people staring at him, whispering . . .

All around him he could hear voices. "That's the one, the new kid over there. Scored twenty out of twenty on old Foxy's mental maths test."

"Flattened Basher Briggs without even getting out of breath!"

"Did this brilliant cartoon of old Hughes in *seconds* . . . "

Jonathan was sitting at the end of a table with Tim, who seemed quite proud of his new friend's fame. But he was puzzled too . . .

"You know," he said suddenly, "several times today I thought I'd caught a glimpse of a sort of . . . shadow, or something near you."

"How do you mean?" asked Jonathan, alarmed.

"A sort of . . . shape. That's it, a ghostly shape . . . But as soon as I fixed my eye on it it disappeared."

Jonathan remembered what Dave had said earlier, about only a few people seeing ghosts. Tim must be at least a little bit sensitive . . .

A tall snotty-looking boy in a prefect's blazer came up to them.

"You Dent, the new kid? I'm Hadley, Captain of Games. There's a football match this afternoon, and you're playing. You any good?"

"Just average," said Jonathan modestly. As a matter of fact he was a pretty decent football player, but he wasn't going to start drawing attention to himself. There'd been quite enough of that already.

"You can start in the H and H Team then," said Hadley. "If you're any good you can try out for one of the proper teams later." He marched away.

"Wednesday afternoon's always Games afternoon," explained Tim.

Jonathan nodded. Maybe he could keep out of trouble for a bit.

"What's the H and H Team then?"

"Well, there are three *proper* teams," explained Tim. "First Team, Second Team, Third Team . . . then there's H and H. That's my team.

"But what does H and H stand for?"

"Hopeless and Helpless," explained Tim almost proudly. "All the ones with short sight, short breath and two left feet. I'm Vice-captain."

"Who do we play then?"

"One of the three teams. We draw lots at the beginning of the afternoon."

"That doesn't sound very fair."

"Doesn't make much difference," said Timmy cheerfully. "We always lose anyway. When it's the First Team we just lose by more goals! Forty-eight – nil last time."

Jonathan shuddered. "How did you do with the Second Eleven?"

"Twenty-three – nil, to them."

"And against the Third?"

"We lost five–one."

"At least you scored a goal."

Tim shook his head. "Their goalie scored an own goal. They're almost as bad as we are!"

Jonathan sighed. It didn't look as if it was going to be a very exciting game of football.

But that was just where he was wrong . . .

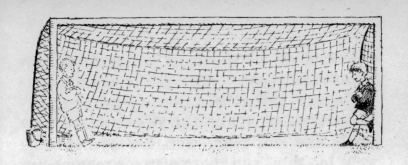

CHAPTER FOUR
The Footballing Phantom

Jonathan hadn't brought any kit to school with him, but that wasn't enough to get him off. Mr Mills the games master, a burly, moustached figure in shorts and sweater, never seen without a whistle hanging round his neck, kitted him out from the lost property box.

Wearing baggy shorts and an ill-fitting pair of boots, Jonathan lumbered out onto the field, feeling a proper twit.

Which was probably fair enough, thought Jonathan, since he was turning out with a pretty twittish team.

The Hopeless and Helpless Team was a

collection of all the least athletic boys in Jonathan's year.

The very tall – there was one gangling six-footer who looked like a giraffe – and the very small, like Tim. Some were too fat and some were too thin, and there were as many pairs of glasses in sight as pairs of football boots.

All four teams finally gathered outside the changing-rooms, and Mr Mills stood on a bench and blew his whistle for silence. "All right, you lot, gather round!" He put four peices of paper into a cap, shook it about, then took one peice out. "This week the Second

Team will play . . ." he took another piece out and looked at it . . . "the Third Team!"

There were cheers from the crowd, and the two teams moved away to the far pitch. "Which means, of course," Mr Mills went on, "that the First Team will play the Hopeless and Helpless!" Groans, cheers and whistles from the crowd.

"That's the worst possible draw," whispered Tim. "The Second and Third teams get a good game and we get slaughtered!"

As the teams made their way onto the pitch the Captain of the First Team, who was none other than Hadley the Captain of Games, said, "You can stick the new kid in goal. He might be a bit less of a disaster than the rest of you."

The H and H Captain, a very tall, skinny boy called Sutton, said meekly, "Yes Hadley, if you say so. Dent, you're in goal."

Seething quietly, Jonathan went and took his place, and the other players took theirs.

Mr Mills blew his whistle, tossed the ball in the air, then went off to referee the other game.

In goal, Jonathan braced himself for the

attack.

It wasn't long in coming.

The First Team took effortless possession of the ball, passed it gently down the field, and the right winger volleyed it across to the centre-forward who drove it hard at the goal. Jonathan stopped it, and booted it hard down the field.

But the ball was soon back before Jonathan's goal, and he blocked another attempt and then another.

Cheers went up from Jonathan's team.

The First Team attackers really started piling on the pressure, and soon Jonathan was facing attack from all sides.

He handed off the next attempt with a spectacular dive, but the ball was soon back in play, and before he could get to his feet, another shot was winging its way towards the far corner of the goal . . . Desperately Jonathan scrambled towards it.

It was quite obvious he was going to be too late, but somehow the ball seemed to hover in the air for a moment.

He only managed to touch it with his fingers, but the ball suddenly shot away from

the goal at tremendous speed, leaving the First Team attackers scrambling after it.

Grinning to himself, Jonathan scrambled to his feet. He had a pretty good idea what was happening, but this time he was quite pleased about it. It would do that stroppy First Team good to have some of the conceit knocked out of them!

As if to confirm his suspicions, Dave appeared in front of the goal, booted the ball away from a baffled First Team attacker – to whom he was still invisible of course – gave Jonathan a thumbs-up sign and vanished.

(Perhaps playing football and materialising both at once was just too tiring, thought Jonathan.)

From then on nothing went right for the First Team.

They just couldn't get the ball near the H and H goal very often, or keep it there when they did.

Most of their passes seemed to go astray, they fell over each other, mis-kicked and just generally went to pieces.

Whenever they did manage to get a shot at goal the ball veered mysteriously off-course at the last minute, going above, around and behind the goal, bouncing off the goalposts and crossbar, and going anywhere in fact but in the net.

By the end of the first half they were worn out, puzzled and cross. Mr Mills came over to see them. "What's the score?"

"Nil – nil," said Hadley grimly.

"What?" Mr Mills was amazed.

"Don't worry, sir," said Hadley. "Things are going to be very different in the second half!"

They were, too. They were worse!

Just before the end of half-time, Sutton came loping up to Jonathan. "Right, I'll take goal this time, Dent. You're playing centre-forward."

"I'm not sure if that's a good idea," said Jonathan hurriedly.

"Oh yes it is. You were terrific in goal, and now I've got a decent player for once I'm not going to waste him. They'll put you in the First Team next match sure as anything, but while you're here, maybe you can score a goal for us, just for once!"

Jonathan shrugged. "All right, I'll do my

best."

But he didn't really have to do very much at all.

As soon as the second half got going, the ball was at his feet. Jonathan booted it in the general direction of the opposition goal and trotted after it.

Seconds later it dropped back at his feet in the same mysterious fashion, and he kicked it again.

A couple more kicks and Jonathan found himself in front of the goal mouth, facing a furious semi-circle of defenders. They were practically standing shoulder to shoulder.

Jonathan kicked the ball straight up in the air and it soared over their heads, swerved past a bewildered goal keeper, and thudded into the back of the net!

The angry goalkeeper retrieved it and booted it right down the field almost to the H and H goal.

It was useless.

The ball flew back up the field to Jonathan's feet, and he took another shot at goal.

The goalkeeper got to it in plenty of time for a save, but the ball paused, made a sharp

right angle turn and shot into the net.

And so it went on.

Wherever Jonathan went, and whatever the First Team players tried to do, the ball always landed back at Jonathan's feet.

All he had to do was kick it vaguely in the direction of the enemy goal and follow it up.

Sooner or later he found himself with a shot at goal, and every shot he tried landed in the net – no matter how many defenders tried to get in the way, no matter how hard the goalie tried to make a save . . .

When Mr Mills ambled over at the end of the game and asked Hadley the score Hadley said, tight-lipped, "Twenty-three–nil, sir."

Mr Mills laughed. "That sounds more like it. Found your form again, did you?"

"Not exactly, sir. It's twenty-three–nil to

them!"

He waved in unbelieving horror at the Hopeless and Helpless Team, who were carrying Jonathan shoulder-high back to the changing-rooms.

Mr Mills chewed at his moustache, a habit of his when baffled.

"I take it that new boy, Dent, scored most of these goals?"

"He scored all of them, sir," said Hadley bitterly. "Every single one. And what really hurts is, I put him on their team!"

CHAPTER FIVE
Into the Past

Things were still being sorted out when Jonathan got home, and his mother gave him tea and toast in the new kitchen, with familiar objects – cups and plates and pans and cutlery – spread out higgledy-piggledy in unfamiliar surroundings.

"How was your first day at school?" she asked.

Jonathan took a swig of tea. "Interesting . . ."

"You look a bit tired."

"Well, there was quite a lot going on, you know . . ."

Which was the understatement of the

century, thought Jonathan.

Suddenly there was a ring at the doorbell.

His mother went to answer it, and returned with a large overpowering woman in a tweed suit. "This is Mrs Maylie from next door, Jonathan. She's just popped in to . . . " Jonathan's mother trailed off, as if she couldn't quite think why Mrs Maylie *had* popped in.

"So this is your little boy," said Mrs Maylie. "How sweet! An only child?" She wagged a playful finger at Jonathan. "We must see you don't get spoiled, young man!"

Jonathan gave his mother a horrified look. She smiled apologetically.

"Say hello to Mrs Maylie, Jonathan. It's very kind of her to pop in and see how we're getting on."

"Hello," muttered Jonathan, and went back to his tea and toast.

Mrs Maylie looked round the still cluttered kitchen. "Still lots to do, I see. Still, it does take time to get a home really nice, doesn't it?" You could see by her expression that she didn't think Jonathan's mother was ever going to manage it.

Jonathan's mother was beginning to look as cross as Jonathan, but she forced herself to be polite. "Do have a cup of tea while you're here. There are some biscuits somewhere..."

She lifted some folded curtains off a chair so Mrs Maylie could sit down.

"I do think it's so brave of you, moving in here," said Mrs Maylie. "It was empty for ages, you know, because of all these silly rumours about it being haunted. I mean, no sensible person believes in ghosts."

Suddenly Jonathan's eyes widened in horror.

Dave had appeared, perched on the table close to Mrs Maylie. He crossed his eyes, stuck his tongue out and thumbed his nose at her. Then he vanished again.

Jonathan burst out laughing, his mother looked puzzled, and Mrs Maylie looked offended. "There's nothing funny about it," she said huffily. "The last people here had all sorts of silly tales about noises in the night and things smashing and ghostly shapes. Utter nonsense, of course . . . "

A sudden thought struck Jonathan. "Did they have any kids?"

"Children? No, they didn't. Why?"

"Oh, just wondered," said Jonathan vaguely.

His mother went to the sink and refilled the kettle. "I'll just make some more tea . . . Do have some toast."

Mrs Maylie reached for a piece of buttered toast – and the plate moved away from her hand.

She gave it a puzzled look and reached out again – and the plate dodged to the right. Determinedly, she snatched at it – and it slid to the left.

Jonathan reached out and grabbed the plate, feeling a slight tug as he snatched it from David's invisible hand. "Do have some toast," he said politely.

Mrs Maylie took a piece of toast, and sat munching it nervously.

Recovering herself she started firing questions at Jonathan about his school-work, not stopping to listen to any of his answers.

His mother came back with a cup of tea and sat listening politely as Mrs Maylie rattled on.

Time passed, and Mrs Maylie showed no signs of leaving. After her third cup of tea, she looked pointedly at the empty toast plate.

"Did I hear you mention something about some biscuits?"

Jonathan's mother looked round the kitchen. "Yes, of course, now where are they? I think they're still in the tea chest in the hall."

She went out of the kitchen – and suddenly Mrs Maylie's cup and saucer rose slowly in the air and hovered before her face.

She stared at it, wide-eyed.

It dropped back onto the table with a crash, and she jumped to her feet with a little scream.

A pile of saucepans jumped from a shelf in a corner and clattered to the floor.

Behind her the folded curtains rose from the floor where Jonathan's mother had put them, and unfolded themselves into a billowing white shape.

Mrs Maylie turned round, and saw something very like the conventional sheeted ghost floating towards her. "Woo, woo, woo!" moaned the curtains.

Mrs Maylie turned and ran from the room, brushing past Jonathan's mother who was just coming back with a tin of biscuits.

"Sorry," gabbled Mrs Maylie, "must be going, urgent appointment, cake in the oven . . ."

Still trailing explanations and apologies, she disappeared out of the front door.

Jonathan's mother looked puzzled. "What got into her? And what was all that row?"

"The saucepans fell off the shelf and gave her a fright. Then she dropped her cup, and got sort of tangled up with the curtains on the way out . . . " Well, that was more or less what had happened, thought Jonathan.

"Maybe she was wrong," said Jonathan's mother calmly. "Maybe this house is haunted. Sounds like a poltergeist to me."

"Like a what?"

"Poltergeist. German for noisy ghost. There are lots of reports of them. They're pretty harmless really, they just make noises and break things and play silly tricks."

Jonathan was amazed that she was taking things so calmly. "What shall we do – if there is one?"

"Nothing so long as it behaves itself. If it goes too far I'll find a priest and have it exorcised. That'll fix it! Now, I must get on with my sorting out. You'd better go up and do your own room."

Jonathan went up to his room, looked at the clutter of books, games, toys, clothes and general odds and ends piled high all around him.

He sighed and stretched out on his bed.

Immediately, Dave appeared, perched on the other end.

"Your mum's a bit of a tartar," he said admiringly.

"She doesn't stand any nonsense. You'd better watch your step. You got rid of the last people here, didn't you? Scared them away."

"Didn't have any kids, did they? Nobody for me to play with. I tell you, it's dead boring being a ghost."

Jonathan yawned. "Looks as if it might be fun to me . . . "

"Oh yeah?" said Dave. "Well, just you try it!" He reached out and took Jonathan's hand and pulled gently.

Jonathan felt himself drifting into sleep . . .

Yet, at the same time he found himself floating forwards . . . It was like floating on your back in a dark sea, and having someone gently towing you . . .

Jonathan drifted between waking and sleeping for a moment, then sank slowly into sleep. Faintly he heard a strange, distant wailing . . . He woke up with a start, and that odd feeling you sometimes get that the bed has suddenly dropped a few feet, like a lift. Jonathan looked round blinking, relieved to find he was still on his bed in his room.

But things were different.

To start with, he was lying on a much higher bed, an old-fashioned heavy thing with an iron frame.

Beneath him, instead of his familiar duvet was a heavy quilted eiderdown spread on top of thick grey blankets.

His own possessions weren't piled around the room any more.

Instead, other things, someone else's things, were there – different toys, piles of comics, a wind-up train set on the floor . . .

This was a room that was lived in – but by someone else.

Jonathan sat up. The window was different too — a tiny square one set into the sloping ceiling of what was definitely an attic.

A strange clattering noise came from the window.

Jonathan jumped up and looked out.

A little robot aeroplane with stubby wings was puttering across the sky . . .

CHAPTER SIX

David's Ghost

Jonathan stared at the little plane in amazement.

It looked almost like some kind of model, like a cheaply-made toy. Its engine made a sort of staccato clattering sound, like a lawn-mower or an outboard motor . . .

It looked silly, almost comical, rather than dangerous.

Suddenly the engine cut out. The little plane dipped abruptly, and glided out of sight behind some buildings.

There was a brief period of total silence.

Jonathan could hear the wind-up alarm clock ticking on the ricketty bedside table.

Suddenly there was a shattering crash that shook the building.

Jonathan found himself running out of the room, down the stairs and out into the street.

The street was totally deserted and strangely bare-looking. The parked cars that usually lined both sides were gone now, and there were only a couple of old-fashioned looking cars in their place.

From the bottom of the street, where it joined the high street a black column of smoke was rising in the air.

Instinctively Jonathan started running towards it.

As he ran a strange howling sound filled the air, like and yet unlike the sound he had heard before.

By the time he reached the high street people were appearing on the streets again.

The chemist was sweeping the shattered glass of his broken window from the pavement, while his assistant put a hand-lettered cardboard sign on the door – BUSINESS AS USUAL.

A queue of weary-looking women with shopping bags was already forming outside

the butcher's, and inside the shop Jonathan
could see someone handing over money and
coupons torn from a buff-coloured book in
return for what looked a very small piece of
meat.

A gang of excited kids ran along the pavement, shouting and jostling without giving
Jonathan a second look.

In fact, Jonathan realised, no-one was
giving him a second look. Or even a first one.
It was as if he didn't exist.

Remembering why he'd come out, he

hurried along the high street, ignored by the steadily increasing crowd.

He turned a corner and found himself in front of a house that had had its entire front blown off, so that you could see the insides of all the rooms, like a model with one side removed.

A little group was gathered looking at the astonishing sight. There were some kids amongst them and suddenly Jonathan realised that one of them was Dave. He ran towards him calling out, "Dave! Dave, it's me, Jonathan."

Dave ignored him. Suddenly he turned away and began hurrying along the high street.

Jonathan ran after him. "Dave!"

He caught up with him just as Dave was turning back off the high street into his, their road. "Dave, listen, it's me!"

Dave made no reply, and it was clear he could neither see nor hear him. Jonathan could feel the beginning of panic . . . David went up the street and into his house, with an increasingly worried Jonathan following him.

Dave went straight through the house and out of a door that led into the back garden.

There was a grass-covered mound in the centre of the garden with a door in its base that led into a sort of half-buried underground room.

A tired-looking woman in an apron was helping a cross-looking old lady up the steps of the underground shelter.

"You lot still down there?" called Dave. "The all-clear went ages ago!"

"Well, you know what your gran's like," said the woman. "Takes ages to get her in the shelter and ages to get her out. Are you all right?"

"Course I am. I've been to see where that doodlebug came down. Took the whole front off a house it did. They were all okay though, everyone was down the shelter."

"I think we'll have to go away again," said the woman worriedly. "These doodlebugs seem to be getting worse, more and more every night."

"The ack-ack guns and the fighters get most of them," said Dave confidently.

"Yes, but one or two always seem to get through, and one's all it takes."

"Don't worry, Mum, we'll be okay. I'm just going up to my room, all right? Charlie's coming round, we're going to swap some comics." The two women went into the house.

Dave clattered up the stairs, and Jonathan followed close behind him.

Jonathan was beginning to feel really frightened now. Somehow he'd got trapped in Dave's world – with no-one able to see or hear him.

Somehow he just had to make contact . . .

All at once Jonathan realised how David

65

must feel.

Maybe that was why some ghosts haunted people – because they were lost and lonely and afraid, desperate for some human contact.

Dave went into his room, and began sorting through a pile of Dandies and Beanos on a shelf.

"Dave, listen," said Jonathan urgently. "It's me!"

Dave frowned as if he'd heard a distant noise, then went on sorting.

"Listen, it's me," shouted Jonathan again. "It's Jonathan . . . Jonathan . . . Jonathan . . ."

Suddenly everything went dark . . .

Somewhere Jonathan could hear a voice calling his name. "Jonathan . . . Jonathan . . . Jonathan . . ."

He opened his eyes and found himself back on his bed, in his own room in his own time, with his mother leaning over him.

"Jonathan, what's the matter?"

"Sorry, I must have dropped off," muttered Jonathan. "Don't worry, Mum, I'll get on with the sorting out . . ."

* * *

Later that night, just as Jonathan got into bed, Dave appeared on the end of his bed and said, "See?"

"All right, you've made your point," said Jonathan. "It's not all a bundle of laughs, being a ghost. Why couldn't you see me when I was in your world?"

"You weren't a proper ghost, were you? Besides, it takes experience, haunting people!"

Jonathan said seriously, "Look, I know you were only trying to help me, at school today. But take it easy tomorrow, will you? I just want to be accepted as an ordinary kid, all right?"

"Suit yourself," said Dave huffily. "If you think you can make it without me – just you try." And he disappeared.

CHAPTER SEVEN
Jonathan Alone

Next day at school got off to a bad start.

As soon as the register had been called, Mr Fox said, "Dent, Headmaster's study for you, right away!"

A chorus of "Oohs" and "Aaahs" filled the air and someone muttered, "Now you're for it!" It was a malicious-looking Briggs.

"Silence!" bellowed Mr Fox. "Off you go, Dent!"

Jonathan went.

A few minutes later, he was tapping on the Headmaster's door.

A window-rattling voice bellowed, "Come in!"

Jonathan went in and found the Head slumped behind his desk, running his fingers through already-tousled hair. "Well, boy? What do you want?"

'You sent for me, sir?"

The Head looked surprised. "I did? Now why on Earth would I do that?"

"No idea, sir."

The Head scrabbled through some notes on his desk. "Ah yes, it's about your activities yesterday." He peered at Jonathan over his glasses. "Tell me, boy, your last school, the one you came to us from – one of those special places, was it?"

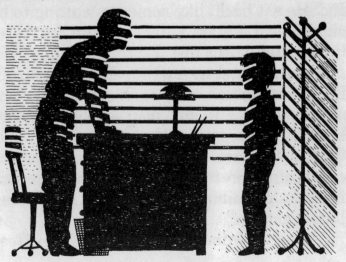

"How do you mean, sir?"

"One of those establishments for amazingly gifted pupils – or for children who are just a tiny bit – eccentric?"

He's wondering if I'm a genius, or just a loony, thought Jonathan.

Out loud he said, "No sir, just an ordinary school, like this one."

"Some rather *extra*ordinary reports reached me – about your activities yesterday."

"I can explain all that," said Jonathan hurriedly.

The Head smiled. "I'm sure you can. Do go on." He sat back, like someone waiting to be entertained. "Start with your full marks in the mental maths test."

Jonathan had never thought faster in his life. "I explained that to Mr Fox, sir. The maths teacher in my last school was very keen on tests, and he'd given one very like that just before I left, same questions and everything. So the right answers were still fresh in my mind. I'm not bad at maths, but I'm no genius."

"An extraordinary coincidence," the Head

said blandly. "And your little dispute with Basher Briggs – ending I understand in his total demolition?"

"Well, he was hassling me, sir," said Jonathan virtuously. "I just sort of saw red and flew at him sir. I don't really remember much about it."

"And the brilliant lightning sketch of our art master?"

That was an easy one, thought Jonathan. "Well we'd been told to draw a portrait, sir, and I'd got a bit stuck, couldn't think of a subject. Then I saw Mr Hughes coming, panicked 'cos I hadn't got anything to show, and dashed off a lightning sketch of *him*. It just happened to turn out rather well, sir, probably because I was in too much of a rush to worry about it. It happens like that sometimes in art, sir, your subconscious mind takes over."

"Does it really?" said the Head. "Let's go on to the last and most interesting item – the rather amazing result of the football match between our crack First Team and the Hopeless and Helpless Team – which the H and H mob won by twenty-three goals to nil."

This was the tricky one, thought Jonathan. He drew a deep breath. "Well, it's like this, sir. I am actually quite a good footballer, and the H and H lot never usually have anyone in their team who's any good at all. They stuck me in goal in the first half and I didn't let any goals through. That cheered our side up, and got the First Team worried. When I was playing centre-forward in the second half, I actually scored a goal. So our lot were over the moon, and the First Team went to pieces. So, I scored a few more goals and, er, we won."

"Twenty-three–nil," murmured the Head.

"Well, it's a funny game, football, sir. You never know what'll happen."

The Head was silent for a moment. Then he said, "Congratulations, you make it all sound very reasonable, you really do. But I'm afraid the sheer frequency of the phenomena are against you!"

"Don't understand, sir."

The Head got up and began wandering about the room. "Well, it's perfectly possible for a boy to score a freak result in a test. Or to fly into a rage and beat a bigger boy in a fight. Or to dash off a lightning sketch that turns

out well." He paused. "Or even, to so inspire a lot of hopeless players who've never won a game in their lives that they score a smashing victory over a very much better side. *But* – " He held up his finger. "When all those things happen to the same boy in the same day – that's a different matter!"

Jonathan kept silent – because he knew the Head was quite right.

The Head perched on the corner of his desk,

and gave Jonathan a surprisingly friendly grin. "I've got the feeling there's quite a lot you're not telling me. Now, there's no question of punishing you. Apart from the fairly minor crime of fighting in the playground, you haven't actually done anything wrong. But I will say this. It seems to me you're a boy things happen around – and I'd like you to see they happen a bit less frequently. See what you can do, will you? Now, be off with you!"

"Yes sir, thank you sir," said Jonathan, and hurried away.

If only Dave kept his promise not to interfere, he thought, things might not turn out too bad after all. They'd even got the afternoon off to watch a school football match . . .

The rest of the day seemed to bear out Jonathan's optimism.

Old Foxy came up with another mental maths test, and by concentrating furiously, Jonathan managed to score twelve out of twenty. Not perfect, but still well up with the top scorers.

"Genius deserted you, boy?" demanded Foxy when the scores were read out.

"Sorry sir, yesterday was just a flash in the

pan!"

Art was a bit trickier, but luckily the set subject was 'A Storm at Sea' and by a dashing use of line and colour Jonathan managed to produce quite a creditable piece of work.

At break time everyone was normal and friendly – except for Basher Briggs, who lurked at a distance scowling, but kept well away. Though Jonathan did see him in conversation with some older boys – and he had a feeling he was being discussed. Still, he thought, Briggs could grumble all he liked, as long as he left him alone.

All this time there hadn't been a sign of Dave, and Jonathan began to feel he might be able to settle down to a normal school life after all.

It was at lunchtime that disaster struck.

Hadley, self-important as ever, bustled up to Jonathan and Timothy in the dining hall. "You're to come over to the changing-rooms with me right away, Dent. We'll have to sort you out some proper kit."

"What do you mean?" protested Jonathan. "I'll be watching not playing. I'm not in the School Team!"

"You are now," said Hadley briskly. "Our centre-forward's got an attack of the collywobbles, too much school shepherd's pie, and I'm making an emergency substitution. You're playing centre-forward. It's a grudge match with our biggest local rivals so you'd better be good! Now, come along!"

He set off at his usual brisk trot.

Miserably Jonathan trailed behind him.

As he struggled into his borrowed School

Team kit Jonathan whispered, "Dave? Are you there? Maybe I *was* a bit nasty. Dave?"

But there was no reply.

This time Jonathan was really on his own.

CHAPTER EIGHT
The Big Match

The start of the match confirmed Jonathan's worst fears.

The other side seemed faster, more experienced and simply better than his new school.

Their attack was fast and tricky, and their defence was like a stone wall.

Jonathan played his best, but his best just wasn't good enough. In his own mind, he just wasn't up to School Team standard yet, and for most of the game play was round Jonathan's team's goal. By the end of the first half, Jonathan's side was two goals down.

In the break Hadley drew Jonathan to one side.

"Come on now, this is a bit disappointing."

"I'm doing my best, just like everyone else."

"And you're playing as well as everyone else too – but where's the magic we saw when you were playing for the Hopeless and Helpless? We need a few miracles!"

"I'll do my best," muttered Jonathan. Hadley moved away.

Looking round to see no-one was looking at him, Jonathan whispered, "David please! I take it all back. Just join in and get me out of this! I'll get lynched if we lose, they'll say it's my fault!" There was still no reply.

Their opponents kept up the pressure in the second half, and narrowly missed scoring

a third goal when the ball bounced off the crossbar.

Then, suddenly they had a lucky break.

The goalkeeper grabbed the ball and threw it to the left winger, who took off down the field leaving their astonished opponents flat-footed.

He booted the ball across to their opponent's penalty area where a waiting forward headed it into goal.

Now Jonathan's side was only one goal down.

Heartened, they began carrying the game to their opponents. Suddenly Jonathan took a pass from the right wing, saw the chance of a long-shot at goal and booted the ball with all his might.

The ball shot down the field as if fired from a cannon, zoomed under the cross-bar inches from the leaping goalie's fingers and thudded into the net.

Two goals to two.

Jonathan heaved a sigh of relief. He'd never made a shot like that in his life! The invisible David was on the field, helping him win at last.

The battle raged up and down the field for most of the remainder of the second half, with

no goals scored by either side.

Jonathan decided Dave was biding his time, not making things too obvious.

He waited for the chance he knew would come.

Suddenly, as if by magic, the ball was at his feet.

"Better make it look good," thought Jonathan.

He began dribbling the ball towards the enemy goal, beating one defender with a burst of speed, dodging another, feinting and sending another the wrong way.

More defenders loomed up and Jonathan slipped past them, confident that his ghostly helper was smoothing the way. He was being a bit less obvious about it too, thought Jonathan approvingly, no miracle shots this time.

Suddenly the enemy goal appeared before him and Jonathan drove the ball fast and low, confident he couldn't miss.

And he didn't.

The ball streaked across the penalty area, the goalie dived and missed and the ball was in the net.

Jonathan's side had won three–two – and once again, Jonathan was carried shoulder-high to the changing-rooms . . .

On the touchline he saw the familiar figure of Dave, jumping up and down and waving wildly . . .

Later, as he came out of the changing-rooms ready for home a bony fist punched him on the shoulder, and suddenly Dave was beside him. "Well done, mate, terrific game."

"Thanks to you," said Jonathan wryly. He

still felt like a fake. Dave stared at him. "What d'you mean, thanks to me? I was on the touch-line the whole game. You saw me, didn't you?"

"Yes, but I thought – "

"You thought I was on the field invisible, helping you out? No, that was all you mate, every bit of it. I didn't do a thing."

Jonathan shook his head. "Well, well, it just shows. You never know what you can do till you try! All it takes is a bit of self-confidence."

They were near the playing-field gate by now – and suddenly Jonathan saw three bulky figures barring his way.

One was Basher Briggs. One was a sort of even larger version of Basher Briggs, and the other was a thuggish-looking youth of much the same type.

"That's Basher Briggs and his big brother," said Dave. "I've been keeping an eye on them for you. Basher reckons he was in line for the place in the School Team, so he's really got it in for you now. So he's brought his big brother and one of his brother's mates to sort you out good and proper!"

And with that David disappeared.

Jonathan said hurriedly, "Dave!"

A voice in his ear said, "Of course, if you're still feeling all independent I'll clear off. But if you don't object to a little help in an emergency . . ."

"There's a difference between independence and suicide," said Jonathan. "I'll take all the help I can get!"

"Right," said Dave's voice. "You stroll up and give them a bit of cheek, and leave the rest to me."

Grinning, Jonathan strolled towards the three hulking figures by the gate. "Good

evening, gentlemen," he said cheerfully. "Been visiting the zoo, have you Briggsy?"

"You what?" growled Briggs.

"I just wondered where you found the two gorillas. You know, one of them looks quite like you!"

With a joint roar of rage, the three thugs rushed towards him . . .

*   *   *

"I see," said the Headmaster in his study next morning. He had just dismissed the battered Briggses and their equally battered friend, loaded down with detentions and now he was turning his attention to Jonathan. "So, according to you Dent, the three of them jumped on you all at once. Yet you seem quite unharmed?"

Once again Jonathan thought hard. "Well, it was like this sir . . . they all jumped – and I sort of dodged underneath them . . . "

"I see," said the Headmaster again. "And in their enthusiasm they just beat each other up without noticing that you were no longer in their midst?"

"Something like that, sir. It was a very confused situation."

"Not as confused as I am," said the Head. He sighed. "Very well, boy, off you go – and congratulations on that winning goal. Do try to see there are no more amazing events will you?"

"I'll do my best, sir," said Jonathan. He heard a stifled chuckle from the apparently empty air beside him and felt an invisible elbow jab him in the ribs. "I'll certainly do my best," said Jonathan again. "But I can't promise!"

Other great reads ❦ *from* **Red Fox**

Further Red Fox titles that you might enjoy reading are listed on the following pages. They are available in bookshops or they can be ordered directly from us.

If you would like to order books, please send this form and the money due to:

ARROW BOOKS, BOOKSERVICE BY POST, PO BOX 29, DOUGLAS, ISLE OF MAN, BRITISH ISLES. Please enclose a cheque or postal order made out to Arrow Books Ltd for the amount due, plus 22p per book for postage and packing, both for orders within the UK and for overseas orders.

NAME _____

ADDRESS _____

_____

Please print clearly.

Whilst every effort is made to keep prices low, it is sometimes necessary to increase cover prices at short notice. If you are ordering books by post, to save delay it is advisable to phone to confirm the correct price. The number to ring is THE SALES DEPARTMENT 071 (if outside London) 973 9700.

THE SNIFF STORIES Ian Whybrow

Things just keep happening to Ben Moore. It's dead hard
avoiding disaster when you've got to keep your street cred with
your mates *and* cope with a family of oddballs at the same time.
There's his appalling 2½ year old sister, his scatty parents who
are into healthy eating and animal rights and, worse than all
of these, there's Sniff! If only Ben could just get on with his
scientific experiments and his attempt at a world beating
Swampbeast score . . . but there's no chance of that while chaos
is just around the corner.

ISBN 0 09 9750406 £2.50

J.B. SUPERSLEUTH Joan Davenport

James Bond is a small thirteen-year-old with spots and
spectacles. But with a name like that, how can he help being
a supersleuth?

It all started when James and 'Polly' (Paul) Perkins spotted
a teacher's stolen car. After that, more and more mysteries
needed solving. With the case of the Arabian prince, the
Murdered Model, the Bonfire Night Murder and the Lost
Umbrella, JB's reputation at Moorside Comprehensive soars.

But some of the cases aren't quite what they seem . . .

ISBN 0 09 9717808 £1.99

Other great reads ✦ *from* **Red Fox**

**Discover the exciting and hilarious books of
Hazel Townson!**

THE MOVING STATUE

One windy day in the middle of his paper round, Jason Riddle
is blown against the town's war memorial statue.

But the statue moves its foot! Can this be true?

ISBN 0 09 973370 6   £1.99

ONE GREEN BOTTLE

Tim Evans has invented a fantasic new board game called
REDUNDO. But after he leaves it at his local toy shop it
disappears! Could Mr Snyder, the wily toy shop owner have
stolen the game to develop it for himself? Tim and his friend
Doggo decide to take drastic action and with the help of a
mysterious green bottle, plan a Reign of Terror.

ISBN 0 09 956810 1   £1.50

THE SPECKLED PANIC

When Kip buys Venger's Speckled Truthpaste instead of
toothpaste, funny things start happening. But they get out of
control when the headmaster eats some by mistake. What terrible
truths will he tell the parents on speech day?

ISBN 0 09 935490 X   £1.75

THE CHOKING PERIL

In this sequel to *The Speckled Panic*, Herbie, Kip and Arthur
Venger the inventor attempt to reform Grumpton's litterbugs.

ISBN 0 09 950530 4   £1.25

Other great reads from **Red Fox**

Discover the great animal stories of Colin Dann

JUST NUFFIN

The Summer holidays loomed ahead with nothing to look forward to except one dreary week in a caravan with only Mum and Dad for company. Roger was sure he'd be bored.

But then Dad finds Nuffin: an abandoned puppy who's more a bundle of skin and bones than a dog. Roger's holiday is transformed and he and Nuffin are inseparable. But Dad is adamant that Nuffin must find a new home. Is there *any* way Roger can persuade him to change his mind?

ISBN 0 09 966900 5 £1.99

KING OF THE VAGABONDS

'You're very young,' Sammy's mother said, 'so heed my advice. Don't go into Quartermile Field.'

His mother and sister are happily domesticated but Sammy, the tabby cat, feels different. They are content with their lot, never wondering what lies beyond their immediate surroundings. But Sammy is burningly curious and his life seems full of mysteries. Who is his father? Where has he gone? And what is the mystery of Quartermile Field?

ISBN 0 09 957190 0 £2.50

Other great reads from **Red Fox**

The latest and funniest joke books are from Red Fox!

THE OZONE FRIENDLY JOKE BOOK
Kim Harris, Chris Langham, Robert Lee, Richard Turner

What's green and highly dangerous?
How do you start a row between conservationists?
What's green and can't be rubbed out?

Green jokes for green people (non-greens will be pea-green when they see how hard you're laughing), bags and bags of them (biodegradable of course).

All the jokes in this book are printed on environmentally friendly paper and every copy you buy will help GREENPEACE save our planet.

* David Bellamy with a machine gun.
* Pour oil on troubled waters.
* The Indelible hulk.

ISBN 0 09 973190 8   £1.99

THE HAUNTED HOUSE JOKE BOOK
John Hegarty

There are skeletons in the scullery . . .
Beasties in the bath . . .
There are spooks in the sitting room
And jokes to make you laugh . . .

Search your home and see if we are right. Then come back, sit down and shudder to the hauntingly funny and eerily rib-rattling jokes in this book.

ISBN 0 09 9621509   £1.99